RAISING
Sweetness

DIANE STANLEY

ILLUSTRATED BY
G. BRIAN KARAS

G. P. PUTNAM'S SONS   NEW YORK

Library of Congress Cataloging-in-Publication Data
Stanley, Diane. Raising Sweetness / Diane Stanley; illustrated by
G. Brian Karas.   p. cm.   Summary: Sweetness, one of eight
orphans living with a man who is an unconventional
housekeeper, learns to read and writes an important letter to
improve their situation. [1. Orphans—Fiction. 2. Literacy—
Fiction.] I. Karas, G. Brian, ill. II. Title. PZ7.S7869Rai 1999
[E]—dc21 98-16613 CIP AC ISBN 0-399-23225-7

10 9 8 7 6 5 4 3

For John, Maureen, and
Bess—bless your little
cotton socks! —D. S.

For my friend,
Juanita Havill
—G. B. K.

It was just another regular day in Possum Trot. I was sittin' at the kitchen table, tryin' to figure out what to rustle up for dinner. I thought about pot roast, but I was plumb out of syrup. There was always tuna-fish soup, but that hadn't been real popular last time I made it. I had about decided on spaghetti with peanut butter when a hullabaloo broke out.

The kitchen door banged open and in come all eight of the orphans—or at least they used to be orphans afore I adopted 'em.

Now you might not think a single gentleman like me would be much good at takin' care of young 'uns. But that's where you'd be wrong. Every dang day I sweep their little beds and hang their clothes out on the line to get clean! And every night I lulls 'em to sleep by tellin' 'em stories about my adventures as a sheriff. Like my shoot-outs with wicked desperadoes or the scorpions what turned up in my boots. Unfortunately, sometimes after they hear them stories, they's too excited to go to sleep.

Now, with some regularity one of 'em inquires as to whether I ever thought about gettin' married. And I tell 'em I did once, but my darlin' done broke my heart and moved away. It's a sad, sad tale, all right, but I can bear it now, 'cause I got them young 'uns. I tell you, they's all just as cute as kitten pajamas, and I love 'em to pieces. Long as I got a biscuit, they got half.

So anyway, them little tykes come into the kitchen, all screamin' and excited. "Looky here what come to our house, Pa!" they hollered. They was holdin' somethin' mysterious.

"What is it?" I asked.

"It's not good to eat, I know that," said Lizzie.

"Cain't wear it, neither," said Pearl.

"Well, I know what it is," said the teeniest child, Sweetness. "That there is a letter!"

It was all full of squiggles and black marks. "What's these?" I asked.

"Them's letters," said Sweetness.

"Now let me get this straight," says I. "This here's a *letter*, but these here is *letters*?"

"That's right," says Sweetness.

"I'm confused," says I.

"Them letters spell out a message, Pa," she said, right proud. "And I know that 'cause I been to school!"

"Well, I'll be switched!" says I. "Can you make out what it says?"

"Naw," says she, and a big tear rolled down her precious cheek. "Didn't stay there long enough. Had to go to the orphanage."

At the mention of the orphanage, all the young 'uns commenced to shudder. You see, that there orphanage was run by a female person named Mrs. Sump, who was meaner than a skilletful of rattlesnakes. She used to make them poor little tykes scrub her floors with toothbrushes. Which is plumb ridiculous, since everybody knows you can get the dirt out a lot faster with a shovel.

But it don't matter now, thank goodness, 'cause I adopted all them orphans and put her right out of business.

"Well," says I, "ain't nothin' stoppin' you from goin' to school now. If people are gonna start sendin' us these letters what got letters on 'em, we better learn how to read 'em."

"Pa, you is right, as always," says little Sweetness. "Exceptin' for one little problem."

"What's that," says I.

"The teacher done left," says she.

"Yes," I answered. "I knowed that. She done gone to New York City, and that's a long, long ways away. Maybe even a hundred miles."

"So they had to get a substitute," says Sweetness.

"Well, that's all right, ain't it?" says I.

"The substitute is Mrs. Sump."

Well, now *that* was an evil twist of fate! It looked like we wasn't *ever* gonna find out what that there letter said.

But then little Sweetness piped up and says, "Looky here, I know what to do. I'll go to school and figger out the readin'. Then I'll teach it to y'all."

"Now wait just a dang minute," I says. "You ain't goin' over there. That woman ain't fit to sleep with dogs."

"Don't matter," says she, "'cause I ain't goin' inside. I'm gonna
peek in through the window."

"Well, now, I guess I'll allow that," says I. "But you ain't goin'
nowhere with your hair every which way like that. Jack, run and
get that fork so's we can comb it out some. Make sure you wipe
the gravy off first."

"Pa," says little Tammy, "you ever thought about gettin' married?"

Well, Sweetness went over to the schoolhouse every day. And every night we all sat around listenin' to her stories about A's and B's and 3's and 4's. Now, I admits I ain't had no schoolin', but I suspect that Mrs. Sump was leadin' them little ducks to the wrong pond. For example, she was tryin' to tell them that if you adds up 1 and 8 you gits 9. Ever dang fool knows you gits 18! It's a good thing I'm here to straighten them out.

And she's got these two different letters, C and K, for instance. They got the exact same sound. Except that sometimes C sounds like S. I guess it depends on what kinda mood it's in. Every night we'd get out our mysterious letter and look it over. We found out it had a lot of A's in it, all right. And some B's and C's, too, though I wasn't sure how these particular C's was feelin', so that wasn't too helpful.

I got so preoccupied with the readin' that I got downright
neglectful. Such as, Timmy's pants had a great big tear in 'em
and I forgot to buy tape three days runnin'. And one night
I let my pickle and banana pie get burned to a cinder. Them
sweet babies pretended they didn't mind a bit, too, just so's I
wouldn't feel bad.

"Pa," says little Kate, "you ever thought about gettin'
married?"

Well, the readin' just went on and on. By the time we got
to P and Q, it seemed to me that we had more letters than we'd
ever need. But most days here come Sweetness with another one.

"How many of them dang things is there?" I asked.

"Twenty-six," said she.

"Well, dog bite my buttons!" says I. "Seems like five or six
would be enough! Heck, maybe readin' ain't worth all this
trouble!"

"I have a feelin' it is," says Sweetness, studyin' our letter.
"I'm startin' to figger this out."

Well, Noah's flood coulda dried up afore we got through that there applebet. Sweetness said the little tykes at school couldn't make much progress on accounta all the scrubbin'. Seems Mrs. Sump was still partial to toothbrushes, y'see. Once she got them desks as shiny as a bald man's head, she set them to work cleanin' the blackboard.

"That's all right," I says. "I betcha you don't use those last letters much anyway."

"Pa, you is right as always," said she.

That night she was studyin' the letter like usual, when all of a sudden her jaw flopped open. Then she lit up and smiled like a pig that done fell in butter.

"Pa," says she, "you got any paper?"

I thought about that real hard, till my eye lit on a bar of soap. It had paper wrapped around it, so I gave her that. I'll be dogged if the soap didn't work much better after that, too!

Then Sweetness sat down and started writin' stuff on that paper. The next mornin' she carried it with her to town.

From then on, she stopped goin' down to the schoolhouse. She just sat around smiling and staring out the windows. Couldn't see much through 'em, though, on accounta the dirt, so I cleaned 'em up for her. I didn't just use lard, neither. I used real butter.

"Pa," says John, "you ever think about gettin' married?"

About a week later, I was mashin' avocados for the ice cream when there came a knock on the door.

Well, you coulda knocked me over with a feather! Who should I see standing there on our front step, just as sweet as a Georgia peach, but my long lost love, Lucy Locket! Now, you remember my sad, sad tale? Well, it was all about Miss Lucy. You see, I've adored that woman since God made dirt, but a while back she up and moved to New York City.

"Why, Miss Lucy," I cried, "I never thought I'd see you again!"

"Well, you almost didn't. When you didn't answer my letter, I figured you'd forgotten about me."

"So it was *you* that sent that letter!" says I, and I pulled it out of my pocket. I tried to smooth out the wrinkles a trifle. There wasn't nothin' I could do about the ketchup spots.

"That's my letter, all right, and I'm still waitin' for the answer."

"Well, you may have to wait a spell longer," I said, lookin' kinda embarrassed, "on accounta I can't read it yet. We been workin' on it right hard, though."

Miss Lucy looked at me all sweet and said, "I'll tell you what. How about I read it to you. That might speed things along, don't you think?"

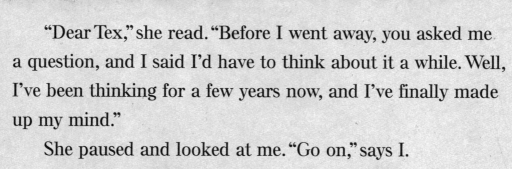

"Dear Tex," she read. "Before I went away, you asked me a question, and I said I'd have to think about it a while. Well, I've been thinking for a few years now, and I've finally made up my mind."

She paused and looked at me. "Go on," says I.

"Do you remember what the question was?" she asked.

"Yeah," I said, and my face went all red.

"Very good," said Miss Lucy, and she went back to readin' the letter. "I have decided to accept your proposal of marriage."

"Ma!" cried the young 'uns, and they fell on her like a duck on a june bug.

"I got myself a family since you been gone," I explained.

"So I see," said Miss Lucy, pattin' their little heads. "But let me finish. I will move back to Possum Trot and be your wife on one condition. I plan to go on working at my chosen profession."

"What's that?" cried the little tykes.

"I'm a teacher," says she.

Now, when all the ruckus was over, we went into the kitchen to celebrate, and I served up some of my famous chili.

"I'll bet you can't guess what the secret ingredient is," says I.

"Catfish," says Miss Lucy.

Can you believe that? Why, that woman ain't just pretty— she's as sharp as a pocketful of toothpicks.

"Miss Lucy," I asked, "you said that since I didn't answer your letter, you thought I had done forgot you."

"That's so," says she.

"So how come you're sittin' here at my table?"

" 'Cause someone else answered my letter," says she. Miss Lucy opened her purse, and out come that soap wrapper. On the inside part of it was a whole bunch of them letters we learned.

"What do it say?" I asked. So she read it.

Dear Miss Lucy.

Kum kwik. Wee need U. Ets a emerjunCee.

♡

Sweetness

Now that made me pause a spell. "Why, Sweetness, I'm tickled pink you got Miss Lucy here. But what was the emergency?"

"Oh," says she, "we just didn't want your heart to be broke no more. We thought it was time you got married."

Miss Lucy went back to teachin' school the very next day. She figured the substitute had substituted long enough. You couldn't get an argument on that—except from Mrs. Sump, that is. She was mad enough to eat bees, so she up and left town. Last I heard, she'd done joined the U.S. Army. They say that since she's been there, them soldiers sure got shiny shoes!

Me and Miss Lucy finally tied the knot, and now my heart ain't broke no more. As for them young'uns, they took to Miss Lucy like a hog to persimmons. What's more, they're all learnin' how to read now, so if we ever get another one of them letters, why, they'll figger it out in no time.

So I'd have to say that everything is just about perfect now. Except for one thing. See, my Lucy's got some right contrary views on housekeepin'. Now, I let her have her way, so's not to hurt her feelin's, but she insists on dumpin' all the clothes in soapy water afore puttin' them out on the line. And she done washed all the butter off the windows, too.

But the worst part is her cookin'. Now I wouldn't tell this to just anybody, but I gotta get it off my chest. If you can imagine this—that woman don't even know enough to put the raisins in the mashed potatoes!

But a man will do anything for love.
And that's the truth!